Quick Reads

The
LIGHTHOUSE SECRET

Everyone who lived in Cameron's Cove
said the old lighthouse was empty.
Jake and Sam knew they were wrong.

Enjoy more

Quick Reads

Uncorked!
Archimede Fusillo

Illustrated by John Danalis

The Giant Scrub Python
Grace MacDonald Baldwin

Illustrated by David Cox

The Red Boxing Gloves
David Metzenthen

Illustrated by Meredith Plant

Race of Fear
Kathy Hoopmann

Illustrated by Stephen Axelsen

Quick Reads

The
Lighthouse Secret

Penny Garnsworthy

Illustrated by Steven Bowerman

Word Weavers Press

Queensland
Government
Arts Queensland

First published 2003 by Word Weavers Press Pty Ltd
PO Box 843 Bulimba, Queensland 4171, Australia

www.WordWeaversPress.com.au

1 3 5 7 9 10 8 6 4 2

Typeset by Post Pre-press Group, Brisbane, Queensland
Printed in Australia by McPhersons Printing Group,
Maryborough, Victoria

National Library of Australia
Cataloguing-in-Publication data:

Garnsworthy, Penny, 1958– .
The lighthouse secret.

For young readers.
ISBN 1-877073-08 3

I. Bowerman, Steven. II. Title (Series:Quick reads).

A823.4

P.G.
For Jim and the boys.

S.B.
To all the people both
young and old
who love to dream.

CHAPTER 1

"C'mon Sam, it's only a lighthouse."

"But Jake, we're not supposed to . . ."

"I'm just looking, okay?"

Jake raced his bike on ahead, up the hill towards the lighthouse. Sam pedalled quickly after him, worried. What would Mum say? They were supposed to be home by now, studying. If she found out where they were, she'd have a fit.

Panting, Sam finally reached the top. He looked at the round white tower. It seemed to go up for ever. Hundreds of metres below, the Pacific Ocean crashed loudly onto the rocks sending swirls of white foam up into the air. Seagulls circled, crying. It was creepy. Jake was nowhere to be seen.

Sam felt uncomfortable in the shadow of the huge tower. When they'd first moved to Cameron's Cove a year ago they had driven up to see the lighthouse with their parents, but had never been back. Everyone said there was danger at the lighthouse and Sam wasn't really interested in finding out what sort of danger they meant.

He leant his bike against the rusty wire fence that separated him from the ocean below and explored the area around the lighthouse, calling out to Jake. When there was no answer, he plucked up enough courage to walk over and peer through a gap in one of the boarded-up windows.

It was very dark but Sam could just make out the outline of some high benches. Then he saw his brother. He was there all right, walking around inside!

Sam yelled out to Jake, but he didn't hear him. This wasn't right, he knew it. What if they got caught? The lighthouse wasn't open to the public any more. They were still trespassing. The wooden door creaked and groaned as he pushed it slowly open and peered inside.

"Jake?" he whispered, then jumped in fright as Jake appeared a few metres in front of him and beckoned him over.

"The door was open so I just came in," Jake whispered back. "No one's here."

"Then why are we whispering?" Sam asked. But he didn't raise his voice.

Jake rolled his eyes and started to walk around the room.

A cold shiver ran down Sam's spine as he followed his brother in the half dark through the maze of benches. There were a dozen or more, about chest height, and they were covered in all sorts of equipment. He was careful not to touch anything, afraid he might knock over one of the many glass containers filled with liquid.

"I wonder what sort of experiments these are?" Jake said quietly.

His voice seemed to echo in the round room, but its sound gave them both more confidence.

"Experiments?" Sam gulped. "What do you mean?"

"Well, with all this scientific stuff,

someone must be doing experiments,"
Jake replied knowingly and walked away.

"Where are you going?" Sam said
urgently.

Jake pointed to the far wall. "I'm thirsty
after all that cycling and there's a fridge."

"Jake, let's get out of here," urged Sam,
but Jake was already opening the
refrigerator door.

"Hey, there's juices in here—they're not
labelled, but it looks like orange,
pineapple and that blackcurrant stuff
Mum buys. Want some?"

"No! This is someone else's fridge, not
ours."

"But the door was open—maybe they
leave it open so people like us can come
in and have a drink."

"I don't think so. Let's just go."

But Jake was already taking a bottle out of the refrigerator. As he stuffed it in his pocket a voice boomed out across the room.

"Hey, what are you two doing there?"

Jake backed hastily away from the refrigerator. The door slammed shut and Sam gave a small high-pitched cry.

The voice belonged to a very old, very tall man who wore dirty grey overalls. His gold-rimmed spectacles were cracked and his grey beard fell all the way to his chest. Jake and Sam froze as he walked towards them.

"You shouldn't be in here you know. It's private property," the old man said gruffly.

"The door w-was open," Jake stuttered. Sam was shaking too much to speak.

"Well, never mind then, off with you
both."

They didn't need any more
encouragement to leave. Quickly they ran
between the benches, out the door and
over to their bikes.

"That was creepy!" Sam gasped.

Jake pulled the bottle from his pocket and started to open it.

"Exciting though, wasn't it?" he said. "Want some orange juice?"

"No! We shouldn't have gone in there—and you shouldn't have taken that bottle! It's stealing, and you can't drink that stuff. It could be poisonous."

"Smell it. It's only orange juice," Jake said, as he took a swig. "That old man won't miss one bottle."

Sam stared at his brother in horror as he downed the juice. Why did he always have to show off like this? Just because he was older he thought he knew everything.

"It doesn't taste very nice," Jake said, making a face as he wiped his mouth.

"C'mon. Mum'll be mad when she finds out we're not home. I've got homework to do before dinner, even if you don't."

Little brothers spoil everything Jake thought, as he jumped on his bike. He threw the empty bottle into a nearby rubbish bin and followed his brother down the hill. He wished Sam was more

adventurous. He had to admit Sam was a pretty good surfer, but he was very cautious. Always thinking about what might go wrong.

Without realising it Jake had overtaken Sam, and within seconds he was way out in front.

Jake sped down Central Avenue in record time and turned into his own street. His bike seemed to be unstoppable. He hadn't been pedalling any faster than usual, but he'd made it home unbelievably quickly. He jumped off his bike and examined it thoroughly, looking for something different. He couldn't understand it. The bike looked exactly the same as usual. If anything, his legs felt different, loose and light. Weird.

CHAPTER 2

"What did you race off like that for?" Sam complained as he pulled up at the back gate.

"I couldn't help it—it was like my bike had a mind of its own."

"Yeah, right Jake!" Sam stacked his bike up against the garage and they walked up to the house. They could hear Mum around the corner, hanging out the washing with the radio on. They yelled out to let her know they were home and then opened the back door.

Sam went straight to the fridge for

some iced water while Jake headed for the stairs. Maybe he could slip in a computer game or two before starting his homework—he hated studying. He took the stairs two at a time as usual, but went too fast and landed with a thud on the top landing.

"What was that?" Sam called from the kitchen.

Jake was already at his bedroom door. What's happening to me? he asked himself, looking back. It had taken him no longer than a second to reach the top of the stairs, and less to get to his bedroom door. Fortunately his room was at the end of the hall, or he would have gone straight past it, he'd been moving so quickly.

He was still looking at the stairs when

Sam appeared at the top. "Hey, are you okay?" he asked.

"I don't know," said Jake vaguely. "Everything's really strange—I can't seem to walk slowly any more."

"What?" Sam said, his face scrunched up in confusion.

Jake slowly turned towards his bedroom door and stepped carefully inside.

Immediately he found himself standing at his desk. Weird! He turned on his computer—he didn't want to think about it.

As he sat down at his desk and opened his history book, Sam stared out of his bedroom window towards the coast.

He could just see the tip of the lighthouse
way off in the distance.

I wonder why it's dangerous over there?
Maybe it's something to do with that old
man. He was a bit scary . . . but then he
was angry because we'd gone inside
without asking. Anyone would've been.

And it had been a bit of an adventure this afternoon, he had to admit that.

He didn't usually do stuff with Jake— they were so different. Jake played football and went skate boarding. Sam preferred to go to the beach, where he'd surf, swim or just read a book. And he enjoyed school. He knew Jake thought he was boring, which was why he'd gone with him to the lighthouse. Maybe Jake might change his mind a bit now.

"Finished your homework yet, Jake?" Mrs Clayton called from the staircase.

Sam grinned. Mum never asked him— she knew he would have. But he guessed Jake was playing computer games, as he did every afternoon until Mum checked up on him.

Jake quickly turned off the computer

and threw his school books on the desk.

"Almost," he lied. If he was caught playing computer games before studying, he'd be grounded for at least a week. Two lucky escapes in one day, he thought, first the old man and now Mum.

Towards dinner time Jake started feeling nauseous. At lunchtime he'd swapped his sandwich for Andrew's sausage roll. Now he'd have to tell Mum. He wandered downstairs to the kitchen, ready to face the music.

"What did you eat?" asked Mrs Clayton, when Jake complained of feeling sick.

"Only a sausage roll," he replied, holding his stomach.

"Well, you'd better take some of this," she said, filling a medicine glass with white liquid and handing it to him.

"Jake, you know those hot packaged foods at the school canteen upset your stomach." Jake held his nose and swallowed the vile mixture.

"Gross," he said. "I'm not hungry, Mum. Can I just go and lie down? Maybe I could eat something later?"

"All right," Mrs Clayton said, looking concerned, "but no more sausage rolls, okay?"

"Yeah, okay," he replied as he climbed back up the stairs to his room. At least I'm walking normally again, he thought as he passed Sam on the way down.

"You look awful," Sam said.

"Thanks," he grimaced, and went into his bedroom.

CHAPTER 3

Sam sat down at the kitchen table.

"Hi Sam, where's Jake?" asked his father as he came through the back door and put his briefcase on the kitchen bench.

"He isn't feeling well—he's upstairs."

"Is that right?" Mr Clayton said.

"I keep telling the boys only to eat the school lunches I pack for them."

"But sandwiches every day are so boring, Mum."

"At least they don't make you sick, Sam."

After dinner Sam went upstairs and poked his head into Jake's room.

"Are you really sick?" he asked. Then he saw that Jake's face was even paler than before, and his hair was all wet, like it gets when you have a fever.

"Of course I'm really sick."

"Have you thrown up?"

"Yeah. Three times."

"Did you make it to the bathroom?"

Jake rolled his eyes. "Of course! Only just, though. Haven't you got homework to do, or something?"

"I was just thinking, maybe it was that orange juice you had this afternoon, you said it tasted funny."

Jake looked thoughtful. "Yeah, maybe it was. It might have been off. But I can't tell Mum—she'd go ballistic. Promise you won't tell anyone what we did this afternoon."

"I promise, but let's not do it again."

Jake was feeling better the next morning. Sam suspected it was because on Tuesday afternoons he had footy training he wouldn't want to miss.

Sam had been thinking a lot about the lighthouse and had decided to use it for his local history project.

"Can I go to the library after school?" he asked his mother during breakfast.

"Sure. Jake will be at footy, so just meet him there at four o'clock and you can ride home together."

This morning it was Sam who was out in front. "What happened? Can't you ride fast any more?" he asked as Jake caught up.

Jake braked. He hadn't thought about it at all this morning, but he felt fine. Maybe he'd imagined everything. "I'm just not in a hurry," he replied. "I must have just been feeling real energetic yesterday."

Sam loved going to the library. Today after school he studied the shelves in the local history area. There were lots of books about lighthouses, but only one had a chapter about their lighthouse at Cameron's Cove.

It was built over a hundred years ago and there had been a number of lighthouse keepers during that time, people who lived inside and maintained the light, and the lighthouse. There was heaps of stuff here, Sam thought, the project should be a breeze.

He rode over to the football field to

meet Jake. He laid his bike on the ground and sat down on one of the timber benches. Jake raced from the field and as he passed Sam on the way to his bike yelled, "How 'bout we go back up to the lighthouse this afternoon—I wanna know what that old man's up to."

"No way," said Sam. "Mum said we had to ride home together."

"You're just scared."

"Yeah? Well, you're a jerk, and you'll get us both in trouble," he yelled back, grabbing his school bag and mounting his bike.

"Oh c'mon, Sam, I didn't mean it," Jake said as he wheeled up beside his brother. "The old man was just annoyed because we let ourselves in. If we ask him this time he won't mind, will he?"

Sam looked sideways at Jake—that might be true, but he didn't want to get into trouble.

"No, Jake—let's just go home. It's already after four."

Jake rode alongside him. "What if that orange juice I took from the lighthouse wasn't orange juice. What if it was some sort of experiment?"

"What?" Sam cried.

"What if it was poisonous and I'd got *really* sick? Then we'd have to tell Mum."

Sam was lost for words. Jake could be right. There was no label on the bottle, after all. What if it wasn't juice?

"I just want to ask the old man what it was, that's all."

He hated to admit that Jake was right. Quickly he thought about what he would say if Mum found out. It was Jake's idea—if anything went wrong, he wouldn't get the blame.

"Okay, I'll go with you, but only long enough for you to ask the old man about the juice. I told you not to drink it."

"Let's move then and we won't be too late home."

They sped along the main street and turned off at the tourist sign that pointed up to the lighthouse. Sam couldn't believe how Jake always managed to talk his way out of things and make sense. It just wasn't fair.

As they reached the crest of the hill they slowed down to catch their breath.

"What are you gonna say to the old man?" Sam asked, trying to keep his voice steady.

"I don't know. I suppose I'll have to tell him I took the juice." Jake shrugged.

As they got closer the lighthouse overshadowed them, a giant white monster. Sam could feel his heart beating wildly. "It's creepy, isn't it?" he said.

Jake smiled, "C'mon," he said, pedalling up to the door and dismounting. Sam followed.

CHAPTER 4

The boys stopped and listened; all they heard were the seagulls and the waves crashing on the rocks. Jake pushed the door but it was locked. Slowly they made their way around the lighthouse, peering into the darkness through the cracks in the windows. There was no sign of the old man.

"Well, we might as well go home now," said Sam, relieved. "Maybe he went out for groceries or something."

"He probably lives up there." Jake pointed to a small window half way up the wall. "And he's locked the door so no one else can get in."

This time Jake knocked on the door. When there was no answer he knocked again. Still no answer.

"C'mon, help me, will ya?"

Finally Sam joined in. Together they banged on the old wooden door. Jake called out a couple of times but still there was no answer.

"He's not here, Jake. Let's just go home. It's getting late."

Jake stood back and peered up at the lighthouse, his arm shading his eyes. Sam was already half way to his bike. Jake picked up a small stone and hurled it upwards, narrowly missing the window.

The rock struck the lighthouse wall with a sharp ping.

"What are you doing? You'll break the window!"

Jake picked up another rock and aimed it at the window, only to miss again.

"Jake!" Sam exclaimed. "Stop it! You'll break something and then we'll really be in trouble."

On his third attempt they heard a tiny click as the rock bounced off the glass.

Suddenly a face appeared at the window. It was the old man. "What do you want?" he yelled as the window opened.

"Can we come in . . . please?" asked Jake. He could never admit it to Sam, but he was terrified.

"Door's open."

Jake and Sam looked at each other questioningly. Jake pushed the great

timber door and with a loud rumble it
opened.

'Weird,' Jake muttered.

"Now what do you want?" the old man
asked, appearing out of the shadows.

Jake didn't know where to start, but suddenly the words just tumbled out. "I'm sorry we came in yesterday without asking—and I'm really sorry that I took a bottle of orange juice from your fridge."

"You what?" the old man roared.

Jake reeled back in terror. "I'm r-really sorry, sir. I was thirsty—we'd ridden our bikes all the way up from school."

"And you drank it?"

"Yes, sir."

The old man shook his head. His voice was stern. "You stupid boy. You stupid, stupid boy."

Jake felt the colour drain out of this face. What have I done, he thought.

Sam finally found his voice. "We just came to say sorry, sir. It was wrong."

The old man waved his apology away.

"Wrong, yes. But that's not the worst of it."

"What do you mean?" Jake asked, his guts suddenly gripped with fear.

"That wasn't orange juice, boy! It was part of an experiment I've been working on."

Jake felt even more nauseous than he had last night at home. "I knew it!" he cried. "Am I going to die?"

The old man smiled a hard smile. "I don't think so, boy, but you could be awfully sick."

"I was already, last night," moaned Jake.

The old man eyed Jake suspiciously. "Did anything else happen last night?"

"What do you mean?" asked Jake.

Sam elbowed him in the ribs, "What about the ride home, Jake?"

"What happened on the ride home?" asked the old man.

Jake gave Sam a look of disgust. "Well, I pedalled like I normally do but my bike went faster than I can ever remember—it was as if I wasn't making any effort, like the bike just took over. I left Sam behind and was home ages before him."

The old man's laughter echoed throughout the cold, dark lighthouse. A smile of satisfaction crossed his face. "It works," he said, "my experiment works!"

Jake and Sam looked at each other blankly. It was all too strange. They both wanted to run, to get away from here. But they couldn't move—their feet seemed glued to the floor.

"That 'orange juice' you drank was my

latest invention," the old man told them. "Come, I'll show you."

Reluctantly the brothers followed him between the benches to the old refrigerator. He opened the door and pointed to each of the juices in turn.

"There's three of them, as you can see. Yellow, orange and purple. I suppose they

look like juices, but they're not what they seem. Each of the three, once consumed, will affect different parts of the body."

Jake gasped. The old man continued; "The purple one is for the head . . . gives you extra power in your eyes and ears. You should be able to see and hear things a long way off, and even read faster."

"The yellow one is for the upper body— it increases the muscle tone in the arms and shoulders and gives you extra strength for lifting and carrying." The old man looked thoughtful. "In fact, for anything you do with your arms."

"And the orange one—well, it's for the lower part of your body—it increases muscle tone in your legs so that you can run much faster." He looked at Jake. "Or in your case, pedal much faster."

Although Jake was shaking with fright, he was fascinated by what the old man said. Could it really be? Could those things really happen? Imagine . . . he'd win all the athletics meets at school. Every footy team would want him! Deep down he knew it was dangerous—but he was still excited.

"They are still in the experimental stage," the old man said, interrupting his thoughts. "I haven't fully tested any of them. For that reason I can't be sure if there are any side effects. And I don't yet know how long they last. Are you feeling all right now?"

Jake felt fine, just cold, this whole place was like a refrigerator. "I was only crook last night. I was okay this morning, and my legs were back to normal."

The old man seemed more friendly now. He invited them upstairs to his living quarters. They looked around while he made them hot chocolate. The room was bare and cold looking with just a single bed, a couple of chairs, a sink and a stove. Both boys wondered how anyone could live in here, it was so cold—with only a threadbare rug on the cement floor. There didn't seem to be a heater anywhere, and there were just three little windows.

Sam was reluctant to drink anything the old man gave him, but the chocolate smelt good. Jake took a sip and nodded at Sam, then looked up at the circular staircase that seemed to disappear into the darkness.

"I thought this lighthouse was closed," Jake said.

"Where did you hear that?" The old man laughed, "I've been living here for years and years. I do my experiments away from the inquisitive eyes of others. Well, I did, until you two came along. Have you told anyone else?" he suddenly asked.

"No, sir," Jake replied.

"Well, now that you know my little secret you mustn't tell anyone, you hear?" he frowned at them both. "Nobody must know—I'm not ready to tell the world yet, until all three liquids have been tested and proven effective. Do you understand?"

"Yes, sir. And if we promise not to tell, can we come back sometime?" Jake asked boldly.

"Jake!" Sam exclaimed. He didn't ever want to come back to this place. All he wanted to do was go home.

The old man smiled strangely. "Well, you know my secret now, so there's nothing to stop you. But for now you have to go, I have work to do."

They showed themselves out and as they pulled the big wooden door shut, they could hear his laughter echoing down the stairs.

"Well, that wasn't so bad was it?" Jake asked as they pedalled home.

"It was awful!" Sam replied. "I don't ever want to go back there. That old man is strange!"

"Scientists are always a bit strange."

CHAPTER 5

"Where have you two been?" Mrs Clayton asked as they slipped in through the back door, "you should have been home ages ago. I've been worried about you."

"Sam asked me to go to the old lighthouse with him. He's doing a project on it."

Sam shot Jake a look of disbelief. "That's not true—you asked me to go with *you*!"

"Well, it doesn't really matter who asked who. You're not to go *anywhere* after school unless you ask me first, okay?" Mrs Clayton said, "Anything could happen to you . . . there are a lot of peculiar people in the world."

Tell me about it, thought Sam.

"Sure, Mum," said Jake.

"Now upstairs both of you and do some study."

Jake was even more reluctant to do his homework now. He couldn't concentrate on anything except those experiments. He might be sworn to secrecy by the old man but he could still ask his mates about the lighthouse. Maybe someone would know something about him.

"So no one lives there?" Jake said to his friend Simon the following morning.

"Nope. Dad says its been empty for years. Ever since he can remember."

"Have you ever been up there?" Jake asked.

"To the lighthouse? Only once. There's nothing there. But Dad says it's haunted—people have seen lights in there at night and someone walking around inside. You weren't thinking about going up there, were you?" he asked.

Jake stumbled over his words. "No, I just . . . well . . . no, I wasn't," he replied, recalling the old man's warning.

The lighthouse wasn't haunted—he knew that. It must be the old man people saw walking around. But why didn't anyone know he lived there?

"Some people think it's haunted, Sam," he told his brother as they rode home that afternoon.

"Maybe the old man is really a ghost,"

Sam joked. But the idea made him uncomfortable. In fact, any talk of the old man made him feel nervous.

"Don't be an idiot, we spoke to him, remember? He was well and truly alive."

"Yeah, well, maybe he's one of those homeless people Mum is always talking about."

"He didn't look homeless to me. Not with all that equipment—it must have cost a fortune. Besides, he's a scientist."

" I can't wait to go back there," Jake muttered.

"Well, I've got to get on with my local history project—it's due on Friday."

On Monday afternoon Sam came home from school absolutely beaming.

"Hey, Mum!" he yelled as he bounced into the kitchen, "I got an 'A' for my project about the lighthouse. Mrs Matthews said my drawings were excellent and I did good research."

"That's a terrific result Sam," Mrs Clayton said, smiling. "I suppose I can forgive you now for sneaking up there—obviously it paid off."

"I also mentioned the ghost."

"What ghost?"

"Everyone says there's a ghost in the lighthouse."

"A ghost? What nonsense. There are no such things as ghosts, Sam."

"But all Jake's friends know about it—so do their parents."

Mrs Clayton raised her eyebrows.

"Yeah. People have seen lights there at

night, and someone walking around. We know that . . ." Sam stopped mid-sentence. He had almost given their secret away.

"What do you know?"

"Oh . . . nothing. Just what people are saying, that's all."

"Well, I'm sure there's all sorts of stories about the old lighthouse, but I wouldn't take them too seriously. Anyway, well done!" She gave him a hug. "Your dad will be really pleased too."

Sam breathed a sigh of relief. That was close.

"Pleased with what?" Jake asked as he walked into the kitchen. "How come you didn't wait for me this afternoon?"

"I got an 'A' for my project and I wanted to tell Mum."

"Great, now you have some free time."

Jake said, as he followed Sam up the stairs. "Now you can come back to the lighthouse with me. We'll go after school."

"What for?" Sam said.

"I want to see if the old man has finished his experiments."

"I don't think we . . ." Sam started.

"Oh, come on—we'll only go for a while."

Sam reluctantly agreed, but this time they got permission first.

"Don't forget we have to be home before it gets dark."

"Yeah, I know."

The wind whistled around the base of the building. They pulled their jackets tightly around them and walked up to the front door.

Jake gave it a push but once again it was locked, so he grabbed a few small stones and started to throw them against the window. Before long they saw the old man's face and he waved his arm as if to beckon them inside.

Again, the door opened as if by magic.

Locked one minute, unlocked the next. Strange, thought Sam.

"How are the experiments going?" Jake asked enthusiastically once they were inside.

"I think the purple one is ready to try—are you willing?"

"Me?"

"I thought you were interested," the old man said.

"Jake, don't!" cried Sam.

Jake ignored his brother's plea. "I won't get sick again, will I?"

"No. I made some adjustments. I think you'll be fine this time."

As the old man lifted a bottle of purple juice from the refrigerator Sam pleaded again with Jake not to drink it. He was really frightened.

"But Sam, I'll be able to see and hear really well."

"What if something awful happens? What will I do?"

"Nothing will happen—just watch."

Bravely he took the bottle from the old man and swallowed it. Jake licked his lips. "Well, that tasted better," he said, "like cherries."

The old man smiled.

"But I don't feel any different," Jake said.

"Why don't you go outside and look around, boy?" the old man suggested.

Jake and Sam let the door close behind them and walked over to the fence on the edge of the cliff. Jake looked out over the ocean. Suddenly he yelled: "Sam, I can see *everything*!"

"What do you mean, *everything*?"

"There are ships out there—one, two, three of them, way out! Big oil tankers!"

Sam could see nothing except water and horizon.

Jake looked down over the cliff to the water below. "There are fish down there, lots of them, all different shapes and sizes.

And I can hear dolphins! There they are, swimming through the old wreck. Wow!"

He turned quickly towards the town, "and I can see our house!"

"Where?" Sam asked, following his pointing finger.

"Over there. I can see my bedroom window, and inside my room. Wow! And Mum's in the garden—she's planting something. It works!" he cried. "I can see everything!"

Sam had to believe him, didn't he?

Jake raced back inside to the old man. "It works! I can see everything! And I could hear dolphins under the water."

The old man smiled. "There's one more liquid to test. Perhaps the middle of next week?"

"Excellent," Jake told him as he and

Sam got back on their bikes and started for home.

Halfway home Jake suddenly stopped. "Oh, no!"

Sam pulled up as well. "What?"

"I just heard a car crash."

"You what?"

"I heard a car crash—you know, screeching tyres, glass breaking. An accident."

"Where?"

Jake thought. "In town I think. Straight ahead. And there's an ambulance on the way."

"Are you serious?"

"Yeah, I'm serious. Let's go and see for ourselves."

They cycled off down the hill.

Sure enough, as they reached the outskirts of town, they saw two cars in the middle of the road. They'd obviously collided. Broken glass covered the road and an ambulance was pulling up at the scene. They watched the medics help both drivers out of their cars and onto stretchers.

"I can't believe it. I can hear so well,"

Jake said. "Just wait until I tell the kids at school."

"But you mustn't," said Sam, "the old man made us promise, remember?"

"Yeah, I know. Until all three experiments are finished. You know, it's not fair to keep those experiments all to himself. Think of . . ." He stopped.

"What?"

"We'd better go. Mum's looking for us."

"She's what?"

"She's looking for us. I can hear her. C'mon."

Sam shook his head in amazement and took off for home.

CHAPTER 6

The next morning Jake's sight and hearing were back to normal. He wanted to go back to the lighthouse, but the old man wouldn't have finished the preparations for the next experiment. The week dragged on. The weekend dragged too, even though he played football with his mates on Saturday and went skateboarding all Sunday afternoon.

On Monday he had trouble concentrating in class. His teacher had to ask him four times if he was listening.

Even on Tuesday afternoon at footy practice he wasn't really concentrating and missed the ball so many times that finally the coach asked him to sit out.

Sam was waiting for him on the sideline, reading.

"I can't wait any longer," he said, as he sat down next to Sam.

"For what?" replied Sam absently.

"I wanna see if the last experiment's ready yet." The suspense was driving him nuts. His whole body felt tense. He was nervous and excited at the same time. "I'm going back to the lighthouse now. Are you coming?"

"I don't want to go, Jake—I'm scared."

"There's nothing to be scared of. Besides, this will be the last time."

"I'll come only if we tell Mum we're

going up there," Sam told his brother as he packed away his book.

"Nah, we're early. We don't need to let Mum know."

Sam sighed. "This will be the absolute last time, Jake. I don't trust that man."

Jake ignored Sam's comment. He was thinking about how famous he was going to be once he could tell everyone at school about his discovery.

Even without drinking any juice, Jake was finding the ride easier. Today, the lighthouse door was open. He rushed inside. His only interest now was trying out the third and final experiment. Then telling everyone about it!

"I'm staying out here!" Sam shouted. Funny, he thought, it was almost like the old man was expecting them. Funny too

how he never came outside—Sam had
been thinking a lot about that lately.

"I have news for you, boy," the old man
told Jake, "the next experiment is
finished."

"Great!"

"Are you ready to try it?" The old man
walked over to the refrigerator.

Slowly Jake took the yellow liquid
from him. A tingling feeling went through
him as he removed the cap and swallowed
the juice. Once again, the old man told
him to go outside to see if the experiment
was successful.

"What should I do?" asked Jake.

"Flap your arms," the old man
suggested.

"Flap my arms?"

"Yes, like a bird. This experiment will give you great strength in your arms. You might even be able to fly!"

Jake couldn't believe what he was hearing.

"You mean . . . really fly?" Jake asked.

"If my experiment works you will fly," said the old man.

Jake raced outside where Sam was waiting with the bikes.

"Well, what happened?" Sam asked.

"Just watch," Jake replied confidently as he slowly started flapping his arms.

"What are you doing?" Sam asked. He's gone nuts, he thought.

"Just watch, okay?" Jake said again, picking up speed. Before long his arms were moving so quickly Sam could no longer tell them apart—just hear them. They sounded like the wings of a large bird. Slowly Jake rose off the ground.

Sam screamed as Jake flew upwards and over him.

"Jake, come down!" he cried.

"Hey, this is great," Jake yelled, "I can go anywhere I want."

"This can't be right. It's not normal.

Come on down, Jake, please—I'm scared!"

"In a minute—I just wanna fly round the lighthouse!"

Within seconds Jake had disappeared from view. Sam's stomach had developed a bad case of butterflies and he didn't really understand what he was feeling . . . terrified, excited, upset, amazed, disbelieving, envious . . . all of these things.

Jake came back into view. He'd flown right up to the top of the lighthouse. Then he swooped after a seagull, chasing it. Incredible! He flew around chasing the birds for a while, then started to come lower. He hit the ground with a thump and toppled over.

Sam ran towards him. "Are you all right?" he yelled.

Jake sat up, slowly rubbing his hip. "Yeah, I'm okay. This one mustn't last as long. My arms suddenly got tired. But it was awesome! The best!"

"That's it!" Sam said. "I'm going home. Right now. This is too weird! You could have got hurt. He raced to his bike.

Jake struggled to his feet, his left leg hurting. "That was so cool," he said as he limped over to the lighthouse. "I can't believe it. I can fly!"

He pushed the door, but nothing happened. He yelled out for the old man but there was no answer. He tried a few stones on the high window. There was no response.

He was devastated. He sat on the step and fought back tears. Why had the old man disappeared now, just when his experiment had worked? When would he get to fly again?

Finally, he got on his bike and went home.

Sam was waiting for Jake by the back gate. "I *never* want anything to do with that old man and his experiments ever again! People don't fly," he shouted. "They're not meant to."

"Well, *I* did," replied Jake, leaning his bike against the garage.

Sam shook his head. "It's just not right."

"You're jealous 'cause you didn't get to fly."

"I am not."

"You are too."

"I'm going upstairs," Sam said and with that he leaped up the stairs, two at a time.

I don't care what he thinks, Jake thought to himself. Now that all three experiments were finished he wanted to tell everyone! He could hardly wait for school in the morning.

CHAPTER 7

None of Jake's friends believed him when he told them about the old man and his experiments.

"There's no one in that lighthouse," said Andrew. "My dad says the old lighthouse keeper died there and then the Council closed it."

"There's nothing but a ghost in there now," Simon added.

"He's not a ghost," Jake said. "Sam and I spoke to him and he showed us around the laboratory."

"I don't believe you," said Andrew. "My

dad's lived here forever. He knows everything about this town. There's no one living in that lighthouse."

No matter how he tried, Jake couldn't convince anyone that the old man existed. In desperation he called Sam over to back him up. Reluctantly Sam had to agree with his brother, but the boys wouldn't believe him either. They thought Jake and Sam were trying to make fools of them.

"Well, if you can fly," Andrew said, "why don't you show us how?"

"I can't—I mean I could fly, but I need to drink a special juice first. It wears off after a while."

"Yeah, sure," said Andrew, laughing, "a magic flying juice? Good one, Clayton."

In class, Mr Roberts finally got sick of Jake whispering with his mates. "Since what you have to say is so compelling, Jake, perhaps you'd share it with the rest of the class!" His secret was out anyway, so Jake told the whole story from the beginning, including the flying.

"Well," said Mr Roberts, "I didn't realise you had such a vivid imagination, Clayton."

"But it's true," Jake protested.

The class was falling about laughing, even Simon and Andrew.

"Jake, there hasn't been anyone living in that lighthouse for many, many years. Everyone knows that."

"But there *is* an old man living there, I met him."

Mr Roberts sighed. "Well, it's an

interesting story Jake, but you'd be better
writing it as part of your English
assignment. I'm disappointed this
nonsense has interrupted our class this
afternoon."

"I didn't make it up, it really
happened," Jake pleaded.

Mr Roberts looked annoyed. "Perhaps you'd like to talk to the headmaster about it. That can easily be arranged. In the meantime we have work to do."

Embarrassed in front of all his classmates, Jake slumped at his desk and sulked.

Worst of all, Mr Roberts called Jake's mum. "Mrs Clayton, I'm sorry I've had to call you, but this whole lighthouse thing is getting out of hand."

"What lighthouse thing?" she asked.

"You don't know your boys have been visiting the old lighthouse?"

"I know they've been up there a couple of times. Sam was doing a project on the lighthouse for his history class. He went as part of his research."

"Well, I'm afraid Jake has been making

up a story about an old man who lives in the lighthouse and does experiments in some sort of laboratory. And Sam, I'm sorry to say, supports his story."

"I can't believe it—Jake and Sam usually tell the truth. Why would they make up such a story?"

Mr Roberts sighed. "I don't know Mrs Clayton, but I suggest a family discussion might be a good idea to sort all of this out. I just can't afford to have these sorts of interruptions in class."

That night after dinner Mr Clayton took Jake and Sam into his study. "I want the truth," he said. Jake knew his dad wouldn't believe him, but he told the story once more as his dad sat patiently listening.

Finally Mr Clayton said, "You sound

very convincing, Jake, and yet I know
none of it is possible. What am I supposed
to believe? Why would you make up such
a ridiculous story?"

"I didn't make it up! Sam was there
too, he knows." Jake was desperate to be
believed. Mr Clayton turned to his
younger son.

"Sam?"

"Yes, Dad, it's true—we *did* talk to the old man a few times and he *did* show us the laboratory—and his experiments. I saw Jake fly right over me."

Mr Clayton shook his head. Why would both the boys make up such a preposterous story? "This is what we'll do," he said. "Tomorrow I'll leave work early, pick you both up from school and we'll go up to the lighthouse together. Then you can introduce me to this old man. If your story is true I will speak to your teacher."

Jake smiled with relief. Dad was pretty fair. And since he knew he was telling the truth he had nothing to worry about.

Mr Clayton was waiting in the car for them after school the next day. Jake had

had a horrible day—his friends teased him relentlessly. He couldn't wait to get out of school.

Mr Clayton drove them through town and up the hill. Within minutes the lighthouse loomed up before them. They parked the car at the bottom of the path to the lighthouse and walked up the hill. As they reached the door, Jake leaned down to pick up a small stone.

"What are you doing?" his father asked.

"Well, the old man lives in that room up there," Jake said pointing up. "This is the only way he can hear us."

Mr Clayton looked at Sam who nodded in agreement.

Jake threw at least eight stones. There had was no response. Frustrated, he tried the door. No luck.

"Here, I'll give it a go," said Mr Clayton
as he pushed at the old iron handle. The
door wouldn't budge.

"Let's look through the windows,"
suggested Sam as he went to the first
window and peered through the cracks.
Mr Clayton and Jake did the same.

The three of them peered inside, their eyes slowly adjusting to the darkness.

Jake gasped. The lighthouse was now completely empty—no benches, no equipment, no refrigerator. Just bare concrete walls and floor.

"I don't understand," he moaned. "It was all here."

"Well Jake, and Sam, what do you have to say now?" asked Mr Clayton. He sounded really stern.

Jake shook his head in wonder. "Why would he leave before he had a chance to tell anyone about his experiments?"

"That's if he was ever here in the first place," Mr Clayton said with a sigh. "Come on, let's go home. We'll talk about this after dinner."

Mr Clayton led the way back to the

car, Jake and Sam following gloomily, their heads down.

"Where could he have gone?" asked Sam.

"I don't know."

"Maybe he went to the city, to tell someone important about his experiments."

"Maybe."

"Or maybe he didn't really want us to know any more about them, and he just— went away."

"Yeah, maybe. But either way, we can't prove any of it now. Everyone at school thinks I'm an idiot," Jake said as he got into the car.

What would he say to his friends at school? He wished they'd never gone to the lighthouse. He didn't understand what had happened, it was like a dream.

Except it wasn't. He and Sam had both
seen and talked to the old man. Now he
was gone. What was going on?

CHAPTER 8

A few weeks later the adventure seemed to have been almost forgotten. Jake still believed he had been able to ride his bike at super speed, see deep into the ocean, hear faraway sounds and fly around the lighthouse. He couldn't explain why any of these things had happened and he knew he couldn't mention them to anyone ever again.

His friends believed he had made the whole thing up. Sam came in for his share of teasing too. They had to be content to keep quiet. Life was back to normal.

Until Mr Clayton read the local paper at breakfast one morning.

"This article says that several people have reported seeing a light in the old lighthouse over the past six weeks. The police thought it might be a squatter, looking for some place to sleep. But when they investigated, there was no sign of anyone. Isn't that remarkable?" he said.

Mrs Clayton looked up from her breakfast cereal, "What are you suggesting?"

"Maybe there really *was* someone living in the lighthouse. The door was securely locked, but there could be some other way of getting inside. What I *can't* understand is why our boys would make up such a story. They still swear they saw that old man living in there. There has to be an explanation."

Mrs Clayton just shook her head. "Don't say anything to the boys about this, we don't want to start them off again."

One night, Mr Clayton walked into the kitchen with a big grin. He pulled a leaflet out of his briefcase with a flourish. "At last I've found something that tallies with the boys' story," he crowed. "I have to show them this!"

He called Jake and Sam into the study and told them a very interesting story.

"Today I met the local historian and had a long chat with her. She knew a lot about the lighthouse and the history of Cameron's Cove. She told me that the lighthouse keeper was very old when he died."

"But he's not dead," Jake protested.

Mr Clayton ignored the interruption
and continued. "The story goes that he
had been involved in some sort of
experiments all the years he lived there—
he had some crazy notion about creating
a super human race."

Jake and Sam looked at each other.

"In fact, the old science equipment you see on display in the Historical Museum actually belonged to the lighthouse keeper."

"But what about the lights and everything? Simon said his dad saw lights and someone moving around in there."

"You're right, Jake. The historian told me that for years the locals have reported seeing lights in the windows and someone moving around inside. I know ghosts don't exist, so I can't explain these stories."

"But he was real, Dad—real flesh and blood. He talked to us, he moved around, he showed us his sleeping quarters and everything."

"Well, I don't know about that. But this leaflet has a picture of the last lighthouse keeper. I thought you'd like to see it."

Mr Clayton pushed it across the desk for Jake and Sam to take a look.

"That's him!" they both cried together.

"Are you sure?"

"It's him, Dad—he was tall and really old—and he wore dirty overalls and glasses just like these—they were so badly cracked, I used to wonder how he could see out of them," Jake replied.

"And he had a long grey beard. It's him—I know it's him," cried Sam.

"I don't know what to believe. Life is full of unexplained mysteries, boys, things we will never fully understand," Mr Clayton said.

Jake grinned. "I'll show Simon! Wait till he sees this!"

Sam sighed loudly. "Here we go again."

"Well, perhaps it wouldn't be such a

good idea to talk about it. Don't you have an English essay to write, Jake?"

"Yeah, okay," he said. "I'll use the lighthouse as my subject."

"Good choice. And next time you guys find something as strange as this happening, I want you to promise me something."

Jake and Sam both looked down.

"I want to be the first to know, okay?

"Sure, Dad," said Sam.

CHAPTER 9

The next afternoon after school, Jake
decided to take one last ride up to the
lighthouse. Sam flatly refused to go, but
Jake felt he needed to see it one more
time. He couldn't help brooding over the
whole experience. He hated to be thought
a liar. The kids called him "Wings" now,
they thought he'd made up the story to
sound cool. He kept thinking about it.
He wanted to feel strong and powerful
again, like when he was flying round
the lighthouse.

The wind was howling as he reached

the base of the lighthouse and propped his bike against the fence. Pulling his collar up around his neck, he walked across to the wooden door and tried to open it. As he had expected, it was locked.

In frustration, he started picking up small stones and throwing them at the window. *Ping* against the wall, *click* on the glass . . . He threw more, then waited, hoping. Nothing.

It's really over, Jake thought, still staring upwards. Shaking his head sadly he turned to go.

He had only walked a few steps when he realised he hadn't looked into the room. He turned around to peer through the cracks between the boards on the windows. A shaft of late afternoon sun caught the surface of a small glass object

against the far wall. It was another
bottle, but this time the colour was very
different. It wasn't purple or orange or
yellow. With the afternoon light shining
on it, it was a sparkling blue.

Jake's heart pounded. Another
experiment, another adventure. Blue?
What would it taste like? Jake made a
face and then shrugged. So what? He

couldn't wait to get inside to drink it. But how could he? The door was securely locked, the windows boarded up. He *had* to get that bottle. He'd have to break in. But the lighthouse was so solid. He sank down on the front step to work out a plan.

He hadn't been thinking for very long before he heard what sounded like a window opening. He couldn't be sure—the wind was strong and the pounding surf just about drowned out all other sounds. He stepped out from the doorway and looked up. The upstairs window was opening, and as he stepped back further he saw a familiar face and the waving hand. He raced for the old door.

PENNY GARNSWORTHY

I love to read books for kids—almost as much as I love writing them. And the more mysterious, the better. Lighthouses have always fascinated me—both their history and the lighthouse keepers who lived in them. This story was based on a real lighthouse that I explored.

STEVEN BOWERMAN

My childhood was one big adventure, best of all, my father drove an ice cream truck. Now I live in an old ice cream factory, in Brisbane, that has its own laboratory. I've already found some old bottles, but no ghost!

Intergalactic Heroes by James Moloney,
Illustrated by Craig Smith   1-877073-01-6

Blik by Sandy McCutcheon,
Illustrated by Nicole Murray   1-877073-02-4

Cooper Riley by Maureen Edwards,
Illustrated by Terry Denton   1-877073-03-2

Jack and the Aliens by Damien Broderick,
Illustrated by Ben Redlich   1-877032-00-8

Wrestlefest Fever by James Roy,
Illustrated by Damien Woods   1-877073-05-9

The Red Boxing Gloves by David Metzenthen,
Illustrated by Meredith Plant   1-877073-07-5

Race of Fear by Kathy Hoopmann,
Illustrated by Stephen Axelsen   1-877073-04-0

Clever Sandwiches by Rowena Cory Lindquist,
Illustrated by Kim Wilson   1-877073-06-7

Uncorked! by Archimede Fusillo,
Illustrated by Alan Danalis   1-877073-09-1

The Giant Scrub Python by Grace MacDonald Baldwin,
Illustrated by David Cox   1-877073-10-5

The Lighthouse Secret by Penny Garnsworthy,
Illustrated by Steven Bowerman   1-877073-08-3

Available from all good bookstores and educational suppliers